A Lift-the-Flap Book

LOOK OUT, LION CUB!

Michele Coxon

Happy Cat Books

For my two cubs, Crispin and Sam, with love

Text and illustrations copyright © Michele Coxon, 1997

The moral right of the author/illustrator has been asserted

First published 1997 by Happy Cat Books, Bradfield, Essex CO11 2UT

A CIP catalogue record for this book is available from the British Library

ISBN 1 899248 36 6 Paperback

ISBN 1899248 31 5 Hardback

Manufactured in China

Also by Michele Coxon in Happy Cat Books

The Cat Who Lost His Purr

Kitten's Adventure

Where's My Kitten? A Hide-and-Seek Flap Book

Who Will Play With Me?

Lion cub is bored.
He would like to have some fun.

Mother lion is going
to hunt for food.

Father is feeling sleepy.

Lion cub tries to climb as well as a...

Lion cub tries to reach the top of the tree like a...

Lion cub even tries to fly just like a...

SPLASH! Oh dear! He cannot swim as well as a...

Or as well as a huge…

Lion cub runs fast, but he cannot jump like...

Lion cub is tired and frightened.
He calls for his mummy and daddy.

Mother lion hears lion cub…

Lion cub falls asleep as the sun sets. He dreams of climbing high into the red African sky.